To Dennis, Nancy, Liberty, and Phoebe —K.G.

For Jessica and Emily —N.S.

Library of Congress Cataloging-in-Publication Data has been applied for.
ISBN: 0-8109-5973-9

Text copyright © 2006 Kes Gray
Illustrations copyright © 2006 Nick Sharratt

First published in Gread Britain by The Bodley Head Children's Books in 2003.

Published in 2006 by Harry N. Abrams, Incorporated, New York.

Printed and bound in Singapore
10 9 8 7 6 5 4 3 2 1

Harry N. Abrams, Inc.
115 West 18th Street
New York, NY 10011
www.abramsbooks.com

Abrams is a subsidiary of
LA MARTINIÈRE
GROUPE

YOU DO!

Kes Gray & Nick Sharratt

Harry N. Abrams, Inc., Publishers

"Don't pick your nose," said Daisy's mom.

"You do," said Daisy.

"When?" said Daisy's mom.

"In the car on the way to Granny's," said Daisy.

"I wasn't picking, I was scratching," explained Daisy's mom.

"Don't slurp your soup," said Daisy's mom.

"You do," said Daisy.

"When?" said Daisy's mom.

"On Saturday when we had chicken noodle," said Daisy.

"That's because I'd gone to the dentist," explained Daisy's mom.

"Don't leave your clothes on the floor," said Daisy's mom.

"You do," said Daisy.

"When?" said Daisy's mom.

"Last week when you were going to that party," said Daisy.

"I couldn't decide what to wear," explained Daisy's mom.

"Don't wear your muddy boots in the house," said Daisy's mom.

"You do," said Daisy.

"When?" said Daisy's mom.

"Last weekend when you were gardening," said Daisy.

"That's because I had to come inside to fill the watering can," explained Daisy's mom.

"Don't fidget," said Daisy's mom.

"You do," said Daisy.

"When?" said Daisy's mom.

"In the church at that wedding we went to," said Daisy.

"That's because the seats were too hard," explained Daisy's mom.

"Don't sit so close to the TV," said Daisy's mom.
"You do," said Daisy.
"When?" said Daisy's mom.
"When you were watching that mushy film," said Daisy.
"I didn't have my contact lenses in," explained Daisy's mom.

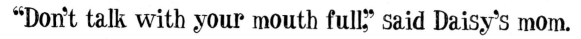

"Don't talk with your mouth full," said Daisy's mom.

"You do," said Daisy.

"When?" said Daisy's mom.

"When your baked potato was too hot," said Daisy.

"I wasn't talking, I was blowing,"
explained Daisy's mom.

"Don't take up the whole couch," said Daisy's mom.

"You do," said Daisy.

"When?" said Daisy's mom.

"Last Monday evening," said Daisy.

"I'd just done my exercises," explained Daisy's mom.

"Don't eat all the good ones," said Daisy's mom.

"You do," said Daisy.

"When?" said Daisy's mom.

"All the time," said Daisy.

"That's because I only like the good ones," explained Daisy's mom.

"Don't keep saying 'you do,'"
said Daisy's mom.

"You do," chuckled Daisy.

Daisy's mom put her hands on her hips and looked Daisy straight in the eye. "I do not keep saying 'you do,' YOU DO!"

"You just said it TWICE!" giggled Daisy.

"Right, who deserves a good tickle?" laughed Daisy's mom, chasing Daisy into the yard.

"I DO! I DO!"
squealed Daisy.